SPACE
MALL

by Jon Buller
and Susan Schade

A STEPPING STONE BOOK

Random House New York

For Vicky I

Breathing in, we lift off.
Breathing out, we are under way.

Copyright © 1997 by Jon Buller and Susan Schade.

All rights reserved under International and Pan-American Copyright Conventions.
Published in the United States by Random House, Inc., New York, and
simultaneously in Canada by Random House of Canada Limited, Toronto.

http://www.randomhouse.com

Library of Congress Cataloging-in-Publication Data
Buller, Jon.
Space mall / by Jon Buller and Susan Schade.
p.   cm.
"A Stepping Stone book."
SUMMARY: Ten-year-old Ron is at the mall when it is hijacked and flown into space
by small but horrible extraterrestrials.
ISBN 0-679-87919-6   (pbk.) — ISBN 0-679-97919-0   (lib. bdg.) [1. Extraterrestrial
beings—Fiction. 2. Science fiction.] I. Schade, Susan. II. Title. III. Series:
PZ7.B9135Sn 1997 [Fic]—dc20 96-25564

Printed in the United States of America   10 9 8 7 6 5 4 3 2 1

Contents

Lift-off

I thought it was an earthquake.

I was sitting in my Saturday morning cartooning class at Ye Olde Mall. I wasn't thinking about much of anything except whether to give Muckman bloodshot eyeballs or hooded eyelids or both.

Suddenly, there was a long, shaking, trembling rumble. I felt the floor shudder.

My pencil rolled off the table.

Cool! I thought. *My first earthquake!*

I looked up at our teacher, the famous cartoonist Bob Elbo, Jr. Mr. Elbo had stopped talking in mid-sentence. He was staring at the jiggling pens on Harold's desk.

Harold Fishbone is my best friend. He is more interested in collecting than in drawing, and he had gone for pens in a big way.

He had two Rapidographs—one fine and one very fine—a quill pen made out of a turkey feather, an antique fountain pen with a gold nib, and three different kinds of Rollerballs.

He kept them all in a test-tube holder so they would stay upright and not dry out.

Now everyone was looking at Harold's pens. They were still jiggling in their slots and making clinking noises.

Harold reached over and steadied them. It became quiet.

Still, Mr. Elbo waited with a listening look.

Then it came.

A tremendous *C - R - A - C - K!* And the whole room tilted way over to the right.

I didn't have time to think.

My chair slid across the room and

tipped over. I fell off. A big pile of comics fell on top of me.

Then there was another *C - R - A - C - K!* The room tilted the other way, and everything tumbled back toward the other wall. Including me.

"ACHOO! ACHOO! ACHOO!"

The air was full of dust.

"Is anyone hurt?" I heard Mr. Elbo saying. He sounded very far away.

I swallowed. My ears went *POP!* And I could hear again.

"There's no need to panic," Mr. Elbo was saying. "We'll go out the back door. Everyone stick together. Are you all right, Ron?"

I nodded and got to my feet.

Mr. Elbo is a fancy dresser. He shook the dust off his gold-and-silver dragon tie. Then he used it to wipe his glasses. He didn't seem to notice the layer of dust on the top of his bald head.

There were four kids in the cartooning

class. Harold and me, and two girls—
Martha Hubbard and Winnie Watt.

Martha is very small. She was standing
so close to Mr. Elbo that her curly ponytail
dusted his retro argyle vest. She looked as if
she was trying to be brave in the face of
danger, but not succeeding very well.

Harold was on his hands and knees
searching for pens.

I didn't see Winnie anywhere, until she
spoke. "I don't see any cracks up here," she
said.

I looked up. There she was. On the top
of an empty bookcase, checking where the
wall met the ceiling. Luckily, the bookcase
was bolted to the wall.

Winnie has skinny legs, short hair, and
lots of nerve.

Mr. Elbo told her we should get out of
the building in case of fire or aftershocks.

Winnie scooted down like a monkey,
and we all went to the back door. I was
first.

Mr. Elbo unlocked the bolt, said, "Careful now. One at a time," and pulled the door open.

"OOF! HEY!" Everybody was pushing me from behind.

I would have fallen right through the doorway. Except it was covered with a sheet of hard plastic or something.

Which was a good thing.

Because I could see through it, and what I saw was THE WHOLE TOWN BELOW ME! About a thousand feet down.

As I watched, it quickly grew smaller and smaller until it disappeared behind some swirling white clouds.

And then I could see the curve of a blue-and-white globe surrounded by the blackness of outer space.

And then the globe shrunk away to nothing.

BLIP! It was gone.

And there was nothing.

Nothing but star-studded blackness.

Under Way

It gave me a sick feeling, having nothing between me and outer space but a thin sheet of clear plastic.

Especially when everyone else was pushing.

"Geh uf!" I grunted into the plastic.

The other kids backed up.

Mr. Elbo pulled me away from the door and slammed it shut. His eyes were as round as Ping-Pong balls, and his mouth opened and closed with no sound coming out.

Then he reopened the door a crack and peeked out.

It was still black out there. We could all see that. He slammed the door shut again.

"What the…?"

He was interrupted by Aldo bursting in from the front room of the store. I had almost forgotten about Aldo!

Aldo runs the comic-book store that sponsors the cartooning class. He is a good friend of mine—and the best model-maker I know.

The store is called the Invisible Planet. It used to be downtown, on Park Street. But Aldo moved to the mall so he could get more customers. He knows I liked the old place better.

Aldo is kind of round. His hair is usually all slicked back. Now it was sticking out in dusty wisps. He was still holding the model of Space Demon that he had been working on. And there was paint on his face.

"Are the kids all right?" he gasped.

Just then a voice came over the mall PA system.

"CONGRATULATIONS!" it blasted.

We all jumped and covered our ears.

Somebody turned down the volume.

"Congratulations!" it said again. "You have been selected to take part in Project Ye Olde Mall. Lift-off was successful, and we are now under way.

"All Earthlings will proceed to the food court for instructions."

"Earthlings!?" Winnie snorted.

Bob Elbo, Jr., took out his pocket notebook and wrote something in it.

We proceeded to the food court, which is on the lower level.

Harold walked so close to me that he kept tripping over my feet.

"What does he mean by 'lift-off'?" he hissed in my ear. "And 'under way'? What's going on?"

"Couldn't you see out the door?" I said to Harold. "We're in outer space! Somehow they lifted the whole mall and blasted it off the Earth! We've been hijacked!"

"Yeah, right." Harold can never tell

whether I'm making things up or not. "That sounds like a good story for Muckman," he said.

Muckman is one of my cartoon characters.

Unlike Harold, I take my cartooning seriously. In fact, I plan to be a famous cartoonist someday.

I started thinking up a cartoon where Muckman saves a hijacked mall.

We got to the food court.

There must have been two hundred people in there. I was looking all around to see who the hijackers were, but everyone looked as bewildered as I felt.

Then a part of the ceiling started to come down. Slowly, like an elevator.

Everybody in the middle of the food court rushed out of the way We all stood around in a circle watching the platform descend from the ceiling.

It stopped about five feet off the ground. And we saw the hijackers.

Everyone gasped!

"Enjoy Your Trip!"

There were three small but horrible extra-terrestrials standing on the platform. They were shaped like warty pears and had lots of wiggly little toes sticking out the bottom.

Bob Elbo, Jr., whipped out his notebook again and started drawing.

One of the Pear Men was wearing a metal helmet on his pointy head. The helmet had two horns sticking out and a gold ring on the top. He stepped forward and spoke. "I am Captain Boot. I am in command of this ship."

His voice was squeaky. His helmet slipped to one side. He adjusted it, but it was still crooked.

Somebody laughed. It was a familiar-sounding laugh. I suspected it was coming from Winnie Watt.

Captain Boot said, "Ha, ha. You laugh. This is good. This is one friendly takeover. We want you to be happy. Is there anyone who is not happy?"

A big guy in a T-shirt and a red baseball cap stepped forward.

"Yeah!" he said. "I'm not happy. And if I don't get home soon, *everybody's* gonna be not happy." He started walking toward the platform with his fists clenched.

I held my breath. Didn't he know better than to mess with unknown extraterrestrials? They always have some secret weapon or special power or something!

But the man kept walking.

Captain Boot smiled a quick, evil smile, like a lizard. "Oh, I am sorry," he squeaked.

Then he glared at the man's baseball cap, and it burst into flames!

The man batted it off his head and slapped at his flaming hair.

"Does that make you happy?" Captain Boot asked.

"Or this?" He glared at the man's feet, and the man started dancing around, yelping.

"Or this?" The man suddenly grabbed at his sides and then at his armpits and his neck. He wiggled and shrieked with crazy laughter.

"Now I think you are happy," smiled Captain Boot.

The man suddenly collapsed on the floor, twitching. Little wisps of smoke still drifted from his head.

"I'm happy," he gasped. "I'm happy!"

"Good," said Captain Boot. "Then I will continue.

"Our home planet is called NAN. We are Nanoosapians. This morning, at four o'clock sharp, we landed our ship on top of Ye Olde Mall and made our preparations. After an appropriate number of Earthlings had entered, we surrounded the exterior of the Mall with an instantaneous protective sealer. This allowed us to lift off, as planned, at 10:45 A.M.

"Your home planet does not have the technology to follow us. Ha, ha.

"In exactly five years and five days, Earth time, we will reach Planet NAN. There, you will become an exhibit in the Greatest Show in the Galaxy, and I will

retain my position as the wealthiest show-
man on NAN!"

"Five years!" someone gasped. "An
exhibit!" A ripple of murmurs went around
the room.

"He's kidding, right?" Harold whispered
to me.

I just shook my head. I felt as if I was
inside one of my comic books.

"Ha, ha!" said Captain Boot. "Is anyone
unhappy about that?"

No one said a word.

"Good. During our trip, you will all be
very happy. That is the beauty of Project Ye
Olde Mall! The mall is full of human toys!
Everything is now free! Help yourselves!"

"Ahem," said a man in a dark suit. "As
mall manager, I'm afraid I can't allow..."

Captain Boot frowned at him.

The mall manager sort of gurgled and
said, "Er...I mean...of course...great idea!"

"Ha, ha!" said Captain Boot. "Money is
no longer meaningful! Enjoy your trip!"

Shopping Spree in Space

The round platform with the pear-shaped guys on it rose up to the ceiling. I guessed that was where the spaceship was attached.

A lot of people stood around looking confused. Some of them were talking in small worried groups. But a few of them had rushed off as soon as Captain Boot said everything was free.

Harold was pulling on my arm.

"You heard what he said. Let's go!"

"Not so fast," said Mr. Elbo. "If this isn't just a nightmare I'm having…" He squeezed his eyes shut and opened them again. He looked surprised to see that we were still there.

". . . then I guess we should have some kind of plan," he continued.

He looked at his watch. "Aldo and I will try to set up some living quarters at the Planet. I guess you kids can have a little shopping spree. But be back at the store in about one hour.

"Don't be too greedy, and try not to get into fights with anybody. It looks like these people are going to be our neighbors for the next five years, at least. Holy cow! Five years!"

He took out his notebook again and started jotting things down. I guessed he had an idea for a comic.

Harold and I made a dash for it.

"Where are you headed?" Harold asked me as we ran down the corridor.

"I don't know," I said. My mind was racing. What did I want? What if somebody else was getting what I wanted?

Harold turned into Speirs department store. "I'm getting a suitcase first," he said. "So I can carry my stuff."

That seemed like a good idea. Harold is very practical. He plans to go to Harvard Business School.

I picked up a big black duffel bag. Harold grabbed an expensive leather briefcase.

"Listen," he said. He was talking real fast. "We should separate. If you go to the stationery store, will you get me that pen in the case? The one with the silver snake?"

And he was gone.

I wondered for a minute what could be more important to Harold than that pen.

But then I saw a lady scooping a whole shelf full of towels into a big plastic shopping bag.

It was time to act.

I took a quick look around, grabbed an electric toothbrush, about six boxes of chocolates, and a pair of cool sunglasses. I stuffed them all into my bag and headed for the stationery store.

At Bobby's Hobbies I dashed in and grabbed a plastic model kit of a flying saucer. Then I doubled back and picked up some glue and some paint and a Lionel diesel engine.

My bag was getting heavy already.

Back out in the corridor, I grabbed an airbrushed T-shirt with a picture of Vermin on it. But I resisted the temptation of the body-building supplements and the telephone shaped like Fred the Cat.

As I rushed past the knife store, I saw that it was completely cleaned out. But I didn't think too much about it at the time.

I passed a man in the window of Pierre-Yves taking a tuxedo off a dummy. I could hardly believe it. What a dumb thing to want!

While I was watching the tuxedo guy, I almost tripped over a tiny kid lugging a huge fuzzy bear.

"Are we there yet?" the kid said to me.

At DeeJay Electronics, two muscular

guys were loading a big-screen TV onto a dolly. Darn. I wished I had thought of that.

I turned into the stationery store.

It wasn't very crowded. I looked up and down the aisles. Most of what I wanted was too big to carry. Like the mother computer with the graphics program and color printer. And the bullet-shaped wastepaper basket.

It occurred to me that I wasn't making very good use of my time.

I picked up a couple of little notebooks like the ones Bob Elbo, Jr., uses and a few Rolling Writers. I stuffed them into my bag.

Just then, a couple of kids went by on in-line skates.

In-line skates! Cool! I rushed down to the sporting goods store.

It seemed as if everyone had been there before me. But I'm lucky. I have big feet for a kid. I found a pair in my size and put them in my bag.

I couldn't lift the bag anymore. I had to drag it. I guessed it was time to head back.

Now that I had the in-line skates, I felt more calm.

As I went by the stationery store, I remembered Harold's pen.

It was still there. I took one for myself too. A cool red-and-black fountain pen. And I picked up a set of watercolors, a whole lot of really good paper, and a beautiful portfolio.

Now I was totally loaded down. I could hardly pull my bag.

I was surprised to see a life-size display monster in front of Pierre-Yves. It's not as if they sell comics or anything.

I was walking backward, with my head down and my butt out, pulling my heavy bag. Unh. Maybe I shouldn't have taken all that paper. Still, it would be great for cartooning class. And the Invisible Planet was just a few more stores away now.

Unh. Unh.

Outside the Planet, I bumped into something soft.

"HEY!" boomed a voice like the bottom note on a piano.

I turned around.

AAAAH!

It was A HUGE MONSTER!

I dropped my bag and flattened myself against the wall.

The monster bared its teeth at me.

Camping In

I turned and ran into the Planet.

Aldo and Mr. Elbo were just standing there sorting comics, as if nothing was happening.

I ran and hid behind Mr. Elbo. He's bigger than Aldo.

The monster stood in the doorway with my duffel bag in his huge fist.

"BOY'S BAG!" he growled, pointing at me and holding up the bag.

Mr. Elbo didn't flinch or anything!

"Thanks, GRUNT," he said. "You can leave it right there. This is Ron Rooney.

Ron, meet GRUNT. He's our own personal guard for this trip."

I stared at GRUNT with my mouth open.

He grunted and went back outside.

"He's not as bad as he looks," Aldo said. "He likes comics."

Aldo asked me if I wanted to pick out some comics for myself.

HOLY COW! I never thought of that! What if some other kid had come in and taken all my favorites!

After a while, Harold came back. He stashed his briefcase in the corner.

"What did you get?" I asked him.

"Show you later," he said. "Did you see all those monsters in the hall?"

"No!" I said. "You mean there are more of them? Like GRUNT?"

"No, all different. Every store has one."

I ran out the door and looked up and down the corridor. He was right! Every store had a weird monster out front! I remembered the "full-size display figure" I thought I had seen outside Pierre-Yves. It must have been real!

"What are they doing?" I whispered to Harold.

"Nothing. Just standing there. One of them growled at me."

Cool!

Mr. Elbo said he was going out for pizza, and did we want any. I ordered my favorite, sauce-and-grated. Harold wanted bacon-and-sausage.

But before he could leave, Winnie and Martha showed up with two kittens!

"Don't say we can't keep them!" Winnie pleaded before anyone could say a word. "Somebody has to take care of them!"

"And we got everything they need," Martha added, pulling up a cart full of stuff.

Winnie held up each item and announced what it was.

"Kitty litter," she said. "Kitty litter box. Cat food. Cat bowls. Toys." She dangled a little mouse on the end of a fishing pole. The black kitten pounced on it.

"Flea comb," Winnie continued. "Kitty litter scoop. Plastic bags. Scratching post. Nail clippers. Cat toothbrush. Books on cat care.

"We can keep them, can't we? Please?"

GRUNT had come in. He picked up the sleepy orange kitten. It lay in his huge, soft, fleshy hand. And it purred.

Aldo was playing with the black kitten. I could tell he wanted to keep them. Mr.

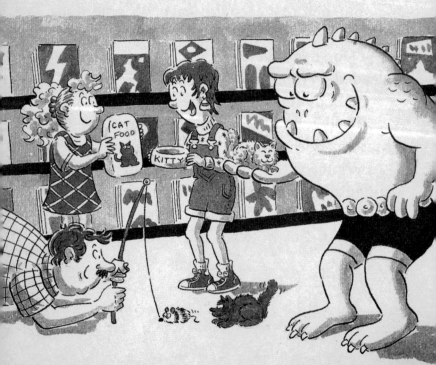

Elbo shrugged. "Why not?" he said with a smile. "In this crazy world, in this demon-ridden mall, flying through space, why ever not?"

"Ooooh!" Winnie said. "That's what I'm naming mine. Why ever not?"

"What?" I said.

"What do you mean, what?"

"What are you naming it?"

"Why ever not? That's what I said!" She took the orange kitten from GRUNT and spoke to it. "Hello, Whyevernot."

I finally got it. I was jealous. I wanted a kitten named Whyevernot more than I had ever wanted anything.

"What are you naming yours, Martha?" Harold asked.

"I don't know. Got any ideas?"

"How about Because?" Winnie said.

"How about BeClaws?" I said.

Everybody laughed. And I felt better.

BeClaws came right up to me and squeaked. "Mah!" it said.

"Want to see what I got?" Harold said.

He opened his leather briefcase.

We all crowded around and looked in. It was full of milkcaps and slammers.

They're for a game we used to play at school. Before it got banned. Sometimes it's called Pogs.

It wasn't what I had expected from a future graduate of Harvard Business School.

But of course, Harold had a plan.

"See, I had this idea!" Harold said excitedly. "That if money was meaningless, then there would be other forms of exchange and barter! And I tried to think of something that I could have a monopoly on. Something not too big.

"I thought we could play, you know, in front of other kids. And then they would want to play too. Only they wouldn't have any Pogs! So they would want to trade for them!

"Besides, I'm good at it!"

He is, too. Harold is full of surprises.

I was sort of embarrassed to show what I got. But it turned out okay.

I shared one of the boxes of chocolates. And everyone liked that.

Then they all laughed about my electric toothbrush, but I didn't mind. I had always wanted one.

Mr. Elbo liked my art supplies. "Tomorrow, we can start cartooning again," he said.

The in-line skates were a big hit. Harold said he might trade some Pogs for a pair later.

I pulled out the silver snake pen.

"You got it!" Harold cried. "I thought it would be gone! Gee, thanks, Ron."

Mr. Elbo had gotten some stuff for our back room to make it into a camp.

The best thing was the tent for the girls. We set it up in a corner of the room, and it was so cool. The girls get all the good stuff.

Everybody got exercise mats and sleeping bags and pajamas.

Then Aldo showed us what he had

brought—a VCR and a TV and some sci-fi videos!

Mr. Elbo finally went for the pizza.

We all ate in the back room and watched videos. GRUNT came too. He seemed to like the videos a lot. And the kittens sat on him.

Then we went to bed.

I got into my sleeping bag and thought about things that I had been trying not to think about before.

Did you know that if it took five years to get to the Planet NAN and five years to come back again, I would be twenty years old before I saw my parents again? And I didn't even want to think about the other possibility: of us *never* going back.

Knife Rebels

The weirdest thing about life in the hijacked mall was how normal it got to seem.

We got up, got dressed, went to the restrooms, had breakfast at the WeeBee Egg, and went back to the Invisible Planet for our cartooning class.

GRUNT liked to watch us draw. He shook with laughter when I drew a picture of Captain Boot. "HNH, HNH, HNH."

I put highlights on the side of the helmet to make it look shiny, and rays coming off the ring on top.

Then after lunch, we would run around

the mall and play Pogs and trade them for stuff we wanted.

The first time we played, Harold loaned me a stack of milkcaps. Then he proceeded to flip them all over with his slammer and win them back again.

A few kids came to watch.

Harold had to give me a handicap. Three free throws.

More kids came to watch.

Finally one said, "Can I play?"

"You got any Pogs?" Harold said, casually, without looking at him.

"Naw," the kid said.

"Got anything to trade?" Harold said.

That was the beginning of Harold's Pog business. He did so well at it that he was able to trade for in-line skates for himself and Martha and Winnie.

Around five o'clock, we would go back to the Planet and go to dinner with Aldo and Mr. Elbo. GRUNT would stay behind and read comics. I don't know when he ate his dinner. Or even if he ate at all!

Then we would play with the kittens, watch videos, and go to bed.

Pretty boring.

At first it was cool to see all the extraterrestrials and monsters hanging around, but you got used to them. The serpent types were really creepy. They clacked their jaws and drooled when you walked passed them.

The worst thing was when the food started running out.

The Nanoosapians set up food synthesizers and started churning out fake hamburgers and pizzas. They tasted awful!

Still, it was better than the slimy green stuff they ate themselves.

Captain Boot and his two sidekicks, Boob and Dood, ate in the food court every afternoon at three o'clock.

Sometimes we went with a bunch of kids to watch from the balcony. It was really gross.

They pushed their lips into big funnels and slurped the stuff right up like vacuum cleaners.

One time, when we were watching the Nanoosapians eat, Harold jabbed me in the ribs.

"Hey!" I said.

"Shhh," he said. "Look at that!"

I looked. I sucked in my breath. Whoa.

There was a group of guys sneaking up on the Nanoosapians. And they were loaded with weapons!

No guns. There weren't any gun shops in the mall. But now I knew where all the knives from the knife shop had gone!

I held my breath.

The guys with knives started spreading out to surround the Nanoosapians.

They moved in.

One of them yelled "HAARANGH!" or something, and they all leapt forward.

Captain Boot swung around. His gaze swept over all the guys with knives.

One by one, they collapsed as if their bones had turned to jelly. Their knives clattered to the floor. It was all over in a few seconds.

I said to Harold, "I wish I knew how he did that."

The guys got taken to an empty store and locked in.

The next day in cartooning class, I drew a comic strip about it. I called it "Knife Rebels Go to Jail."

GRUNT was watching the class for Mr. Elbo.

GRUNT was the coolest monster. He was always nice to us. And he liked comics. Bog Man was his favorite.

He leaned over my shoulder and watched me draw. It really cracked him up when I drew Captain Boot.

I made a jaggedy line, like lightning, from Captain Boot's eyeball to a crumbling attacker. I drew the knife bouncing on the ground.

"SHOULD HAVE GOT THE HELMET," GRUNT growled.

"Huh?" I said.

"TAKE HIS HELMET, HE CAN DO NOTHING. NEEDS HELMET TO ACTIVATE THOUGHT WAVES," said GRUNT. It was a long speech for him. And it got everyone's attention.

"Is that true, GRUNT?" asked Martha.

"HMMMP," GRUNT nodded.

"But why hasn't anyone taken it before?" Winnie said.

"CAN'T GET CLOSE."

"Besides," said Harold, "there are guards all over."

"GUARDS DON'T CARE," GRUNT

said. "AFRAID OF BOOT. AFRAID OF HELMET." He looked all around suddenly, as if he was afraid too.

"GUARDS ARE CAPTIVES," he whispered. "FROM OTHER PLANETS." He hit his chest. "ME TOO."

Then he clammed up and wouldn't say any more.

He took a handful of comics, lay down in the corner, and started reading.

I looked at Harold.

We looked at Winnie and Martha.

We all knew what we had to do.

One way or another, we had to get hold of that helmet!

The Plan

The first thing we agreed on was that nobody else should know what we knew. We were going to do this ourselves!

We started watching Captain Boot every day.

We noticed how when he walked down the hall people would scurry to get out of his way. If they didn't, they would get sizzled. Even little kids!

I couldn't think how we would ever get close enough to get our hands on the helmet.

One night, we had a meeting in the tent after videos.

Aldo and Mr. Elbo had gone down to Ye
Olde Café and left us with GRUNT.

GRUNT was watching videos. He liked
to watch them over and over again. I think
he was learning them by heart.

I was dangling the mouse on the fishing
pole in front of BeClaws. "I just don't see
how we can do it," I said.

BeClaws pounced, but I was too fast for
him. I was getting good with the fishing
pole.

"I know," Martha agreed. "It's too hard
for us. Maybe we should tell Mr. Elbo and
Aldo."

We all glared at her, and Winnie snorted.

BeClaws grabbed the mouse in his
mouth when I wasn't looking and tried to
carry it out of the tent.

"We just have to keep thinking," Harold
said. "There must be a way."

I was pulling on the pole. BeClaws was
pulling on the mouse.

I won.

The mouse flipped back on the line and

slapped Winnie in the mouth.

"Hey!" she cried.

That's when I got my idea.

"That's it!" I gasped.

"What?"

I dangled the miniature fishing pole in front of their faces, grinning.

They didn't get it.

"What's usually on the end of a fishing line?" I said.

"What do you mean?" Winnie asked, suspiciously.

"A fish?" said Martha.

Harold got it first. "A hook!" he cried. He jumped up. "Go fish for the helmet!"

Then he shook his head and sat down. "We could never do it. It would be suicide."

"Well, it wouldn't hurt to practice," I said.

The next day we went to L. L. Pea's sporting goods store to look at fishing poles.

"We aren't really doing this, are we?" Martha asked.

"Just looking," I said.

There was a big selection. There hadn't been much of a run on fishing poles, for obvious reasons.

I wanted to take the biggest pole, but

Winnie pointed out that I could hardly lift it. So we tried them all out and finally chose one that was just right.

Then we went to the opposite end of the mall from the food court so no one would suspect our "Plan."

"There's no way this is gonna work," Harold said.

"That's no reason we shouldn't fool around with it a little," I said.

I tried first because it was my idea.

Martha sat down below with a potholder shaped like a fish.

I let down the line and tried to catch the potholder. But I caught Martha's ponytail instead.

After about ten minutes, she put the potholder on the hook so I could reel it in and let somebody else take a turn.

We practiced a lot and we got better.

We also started a new craze. Kids were fishing all over the balcony. It made me mad.

"Now Captain Boot can't help but notice what we're doing!" I said.

"No, it's cool," said Winnie. "It will just seem like a normal, stupid kid game to him. He won't think twice about it."

"I thought we were just fooling around," Martha said.

"I wish I had a monopoly on fishing poles," Harold muttered. "I should have thought of that."

We switched from the potholder to a china mug. It was closer to the size and weight of the helmet.

Then there was a run on china mugs in the stores. Harold eyed them greedily.

"You can't have a monopoly on everything!" I said.

We got pretty good at fishing for the mug.

But Harold and Martha had cold feet. They were sure it wouldn't work and Captain Boot would fry us.

Winnie was all for the Plan. She had

been all ready to try it out on day number two.

It was up to me to make the final decision. And I might have put it off for months, except for what happened to GRUNT.

NO
TALKING
TO
PRISONERS.
-BOOT

Nerves of Steel

GRUNT got busted.

Being too friendly with the Earthlings was the charge.

He got thrown in jail with the knife rebels.

We missed him. He looked so sad, peering through the iron grating that was across the front of the empty store.

And we got a horrible serpent for a replacement guard. It had a way of looking hungrily at the kittens that really worried me. I think Aldo noticed it too, because he started carrying them around in his pockets.

I decided it was time to carry out the Plan, so I called a secret meeting in the tent.

Martha thought we should tell the whole thing to Mr. Elbo and Aldo.

Winnie glared at her. "And what do you think they would say? They would say, 'NO WAY.'"

"She's right," Harold said slowly. "They probably think they have to keep us safe in case we ever get returned to our parents."

Everyone looked as if they were thinking about never getting returned to their parents, and I knew it was a go. We set it up for the next day at three o'clock.

Winnie was chosen to fish because she has nerves of steel.

I was her backup, and the other two were standing by in their in-line skates, ready for anything.

The three pear-shaped Nanoosapians sat down for their meal. They pinched their loose lips into funnels.

I held my breath.

Winnie let the line down over the rail. We had discovered that a small weight kept it steadier.

I almost passed out from holding my breath. So I started breathing again. Hard. Winnie said, "Stop blowing on me" as she maneuvered the hook into position.

I backed up and tried to calm down.

She lowered the hook to the exact level of the ring on top of the helmet.

With an imperceptible twitch, she slipped the hook into the ring.

"Ah," I sighed.

It slipped out again.

"Oh," I groaned.

She tried again. It went in. She lifted the line a fraction of an inch, and it held. Now came the hard part.

I felt as if I was going to die of nerves, but Winnie's hands were steady.

Captain Boot was slurping his green slime. He didn't suspect a thing.

Winnie tugged and reeled fast.

The helmet swung up off Boot's head and way over to the right.

Winnie reeled it in.

Captain Boot jumped up, yelled "HEY!" and reached for the flying helmet.

The other two Nanoosapians jumped up too, with green slime slobbering from their floppy lips.

"Get that helmet!" Boot yelled in his squeaky voice.

Winnie reeled steadily. She couldn't get too excited or it might slip off the hook.

Captain Boot was standing on the table.

Everyone in the food court was looking up, trying to figure out what was happening.

Boob and Dood were running around in circles.

Winnie swung the helmet up over the rail. I grabbed it and hung on tight.

Then I noticed one of the serpent guards looking at me. It was down the hall, outside Hair Today. It started walking toward me

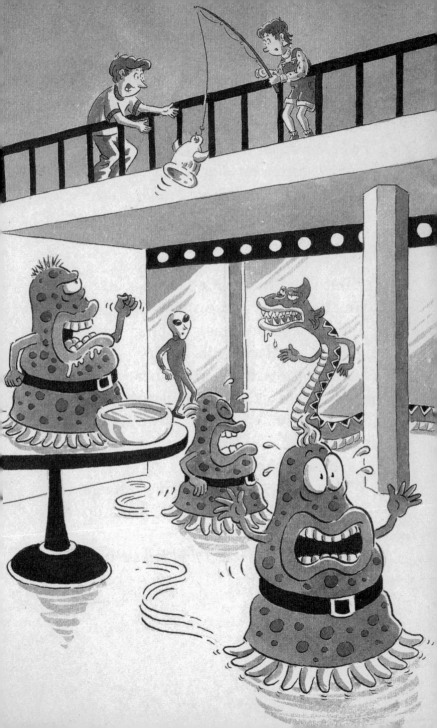

with its claws extended. Its red eyes shifted to the helmet in my hands.

Oh, no! I thought. My mind was racing. *The helmet on the head of a serpent guard would be much worse than the helmet on the head of Captain Boot! The serpent wouldn't care one bit about saving us for any exhibit. It would probably eat us!*

The serpent kept on coming.

But I had the helmet! I put it on the top of my head. It was too small for me.

The serpent was rubbing its hands together and clacking its teeth.

I held the helmet on my head with both hands and backed up until my back was against the wall. I glared at the serpent and thought hard. *Get lost!*

Nothing happened.

The serpent was about fifteen feet away now, and I couldn't back up any farther!

Burn! I tried. *Freeze! Fry! Frizzle! STOP!*

It kept coming.

"It's not working!" I shrieked to the other kids.

The serpent grinned and started drooling.

I looked around wildly.

YAAAAH! There was another serpent sneaking up from the other side! I was trapped! "HELP!" I shrieked.

"Ron! Throw it here!" Harold called. And he held out his arms for a pass.

Saved!

But before I could throw it, the second serpent tackled me from behind. Oof! And the helmet popped out of my hands and bounced along the floor!

OH, NO!

Both serpents threw themselves at the helmet. I threw myself on top of them.

But we were all too late.

Martha had streaked by on her in-line skates, scooped up the helmet, and tossed it to Harold. All before the serpents even hit the ground!

Way to go, Martha!

"Take it to GRUNT!" I yelled. "He might know how to work it."

Harold took off on his in-line skates, with the helmet under his arm like a football. He was threading his way through the

crowd, and Martha was right behind him.

The serpents shook me off and chased after Harold, but there was no way they could catch him. Harold would make it.

"Ron! Somebody! HELP!"

I spun around. It was Winnie!

She was bracing the pole against the rails and holding on for dear life. She had hooked a big one! The pole was bent double, with Captain Boot dangling from the end. The fishhook was in his belt, and Boob and Dood were hanging from his toes.

I tried to help her, but they were too heavy for us. What we needed was a grownup.

"What's going on? What's all the excitement?"

It was Bob Elbo, Jr.!

"Hold this!" Winnie cried. "And don't let him go! He was trying to get back to the spaceship! They wanted to take off and leave us stranded here, orbiting in space!"

Bob Elbo, Jr., took the pole.

He said he hoped we knew what we were doing.

Then GRUNT showed up with Harold and Martha. He had the helmet on his little finger. I realized that he must have known how to use it, because he had gotten himself out of jail! He held up his finger and glared at the three Nanoosapians hanging from the fishing pole.

POOF! They disappeared.

The crowd cheered.

I looked at GRUNT and made a question with my eyebrows.

He knew what I was wondering.

"JAIL," he grunted.

We were saved.

"Mall to Earth . . ."

Captain GRUNT took over. It was great.

He took us up into the rocket ship and showed us how to turn it back toward Earth. GRUNT is pretty smart.

Then he had a meeting with the manager of the mall and got him to promise that everyone could keep the merchandise they had been using.

As a store owner, Aldo said that was okay with him as long as the management would cover his losses.

GRUNT said that was part of the agreement.

I told GRUNT I thought the kittens

would miss him when he went back to his old planet.

"OLD PLANET, KAPUT!" he said. "GRUNT COMING TO EARTH TO BE BIG MOVIE STAR. HASTA LA VISTA, BABY."

"You looking for an agent?" Harold said.

As we approached Earth, GRUNT let me use the radio. He told me what to say.

I cleared my throat and spoke into the microphone.

"Mall to Earth," I said. "Mall to Earth. Clear site for landing. Ye Olde Mall is coming down!"

About the Authors

Jon Buller and Susan Schade get the ideas for their stories from a large rock in their backyard, which broadcasts messages directly to the screen of their computer. They are married and live in Lyme, Connecticut, with their large collection of plastic action figures.